KU-672-037

# Cinderella

## Princess Stories Starring Cinderella

Adapted by Wendy Wax and Rita Balducci
Illustrated by Disney Storybook Artists

CONTENTS

Pleasantville, New York • Montréal, Québec • Bath, United Kingdom

# Cinderella

Once upon a time, there was a lovely young girl who lived with her widowed father.

DISK 1

1

She was happy and kind to all. However, her father felt that she needed a mother, and in time he married

2

a woman with two young daughters of her own.

When her dear father died, the young girl soon learned the true natures of her cruel Stepmother and stepsisters. They called her

3

Cinderella and forced her to do all the work of the household. She sang as she cooked and cleaned and never complained about her hard life. Cinderella dreamed that someday the wishes dear to her heart would come true, and she would find true

love and happiness. The barnyard animals became her companions, and she was so gentle that even the birds and mice did not fear her. Gus and Jaq were two mice that Cinderella fed and dressed. They loved her dearly and wished they could do something to help her.

4

One day, an invitation arrived from the royal palace. "There's to be a ball," the Stepmother read. "Every eligible maiden is to attend."

"Why, I can go, too!" Cinderella cried.

5

Her Stepmother agreed, *if* Cinderella managed to finish her work. Gus and Jaq and the other mice and birds decided to surprise Cinderella. They sewed a lovely gown while she worked at her chores.

6

Cinderella was overjoyed to find the beautiful dress in her attic room. She put it on and rushed to join her stepsisters.

7

"Look! That's my sash!" cried one in a jealous rage.

"Those are my beads!" shrieked the other. They tore at Cinderella's dress until it was tattered and ruined. Poor Cinderella ran to the garden in despair.

8

As she wept, Cinderella became aware of a gentle hand stroking her hair and a soft voice speaking to her.

"Who are you?" Cinderella asked the kindly woman.

"Why, I'm your Fairy Godmother, child," the woman said. "I've come to help you get to the ball." Then, with a wave of her wand, the mice changed into horses and a pumpkin became a glittering coach.

DISK 2

9

Cinderella was speechless. With another wave of her wand, the Fairy Godmother changed Cinderella's raggedy dress to a beautiful, shimmering gown. Cinderella looked down—she was even wearing sparkling glass slippers!

10

"You must leave the ball before midnight," the Fairy Godmother told her, "for then the spell will be broken."

As soon as Cinderella entered the ball, the Prince could not take his eyes off her. They danced under the light of the moon, and before long, they had fallen in love.

11

Suddenly, a chime sounded from high above. The clock had begun to strike the midnight hour. "I must go!" Cinderella cried as she ran from the ballroom. In her hurry, one glass shoe slipped from her foot.

12

The Prince picked up the delicate slipper. "I will marry the maiden whose foot fits this slipper," he declared.

The Grand Duke and his footman set out at dawn to find the owner of the glass slipper. In time, they came to Cinderella's house and were relieved to see that the slipper fit neither of the unpleasant stepsisters.

13

What the Grand Duke did not know was that Cinderella had been locked away in the attic by her evil Stepmother. Gus and Jaq bravely stole the key and slid it under the door to free Cinderella just in time.

14

Just as the Grand Duke and his footman were preparing to leave with the slipper, Cinderella called to him. "Your Grace! Please wait. May I try it on?"

The wicked Stepmother sneered, but there was nothing she could do. Or was there? Just as the footman passed her, she tripped him with her cane. The glass slipper flew from his hands and shattered at Cinderella's feet.

The Grand Duke gasped in dismay. Just then, Cinderella spoke, "But you see, I have the other slipper." She held out the matching shoe to the delight of the Grand Duke and the horror of her stepmother. It fit her foot perfectly!

15

Cinderella's dreams had come true! The Prince and Cinderella were married right away, and they lived happily ever after.

16

Play Song 1

# Cinderella

## Cinderella in: The Best Intentions

Play Song 2

"This guest list does seem to go on forever." Cinderella gave a sigh to her friends the mice.

Though she loved the Prince with all her heart, she did not love preparing for her royal wedding.

"Gus—Gus help Cinderelly?" asked Gus.

"Just don't let all this royalty change me into someone I'm not," Cinderella told him.

Cinderella's lady-in-waiting, Prudence, helped choose a gown, but Cinderella was horrified by her taste. "I look silly in frills...." But Prudence was too busy to listen.

Play Song 3

Meanwhile, Jaq and Gus went to find some help—Cinderella's Fairy Godmother.

"We worried about Cinderelly," Jaq told her.

"She not looking forward to her wedding," said Gus.

"I thought she loved the Prince," said the Fairy Godmother.

"Thassaright!" said Jaq. "But too many royal rules to follow!"

Play Song 4

The Fairy Godmother agreed to help. "That gown does make you look rather like a wedding cake. Would you like me to whip up a simple, elegant dress for you, just like I did for the ball?"

"Oh, yes!" exclaimed Cinderella.

Play Song 5

"Anything else?" she asked.

"I'm responsible for the invitations," said Cinderella. "But I can't do it alone, and I can't count on help from my family."

"We're your family, dear," came the reply.

*Poof!* The guest list was transformed into a thousand invitations, which were sent out immediately.

"Oh, no! The wedding cake!" Cinderella gasped. "I should have ordered it yesterday!"

"How about today?" asked her Godmother. Then—*poof!* There was a wedding cake.

*Poof* again! Cinderella was wearing a lovely, elegant gown, just like her Fairy Godmother had promised.

Play Song 6

On her wedding day, Cinderella felt happy and relaxed—thanks to her Fairy Godmother and friends. They waited with her as she prepared to walk down the aisle. At last it was time to go.

"Remember to smile!" came Prudence's whispered reminder from behind the scenes—not that Cinderella needed to be reminded. She had plenty to smile about now.

As she walked down the aisle, in glass slippers adorned with hearts, the crowd gazed at her with admiration and awe. They had never seen such a beautiful bride. "I must admit her gown is prettier than the one I chose for her," Prudence said to herself.

Cinderella didn't notice anything around her. All she saw was the handsome Prince she was going to share her life with.

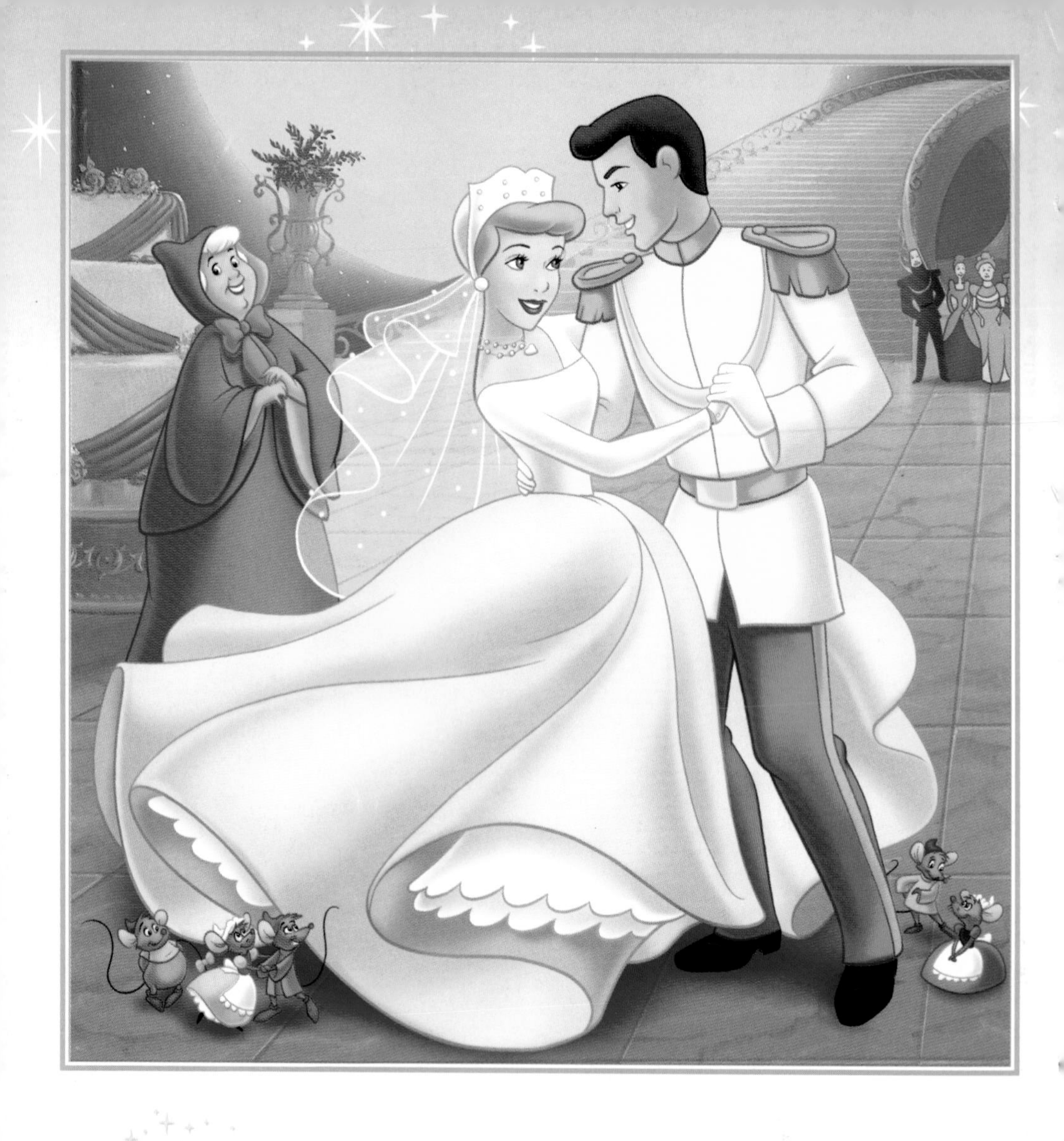

Play Song 7

"How does it feel to be a princess?" the Prince murmured in Cinderella's ear later that evening.

"Amazing," Cinderella murmured back. "But that's because you're my Prince." She winked at her Fairy Godmother and waved to the mice as she whirled past them on the dance floor.